Piggy with the Curly Tail

A children's story by Claudia Verville
Illustrated by Charity Ruotsala

AuthorHouse™
1663 Liberty Drive
Bloomington, IN 47403
www.authorhouse.com
Phone: 1-800-839-8640
©2013 Claudia Verville. All rights reserved.

To Rory
Claudia J Verville

Published by AuthorHouse 2/5/13
ISBN: 978-1-4817-1270-5 (sc)
ISBN: 978-1-4817-1274-3 (e)
Library of Congress Control Number: 2013901894
This book is printed on acid-free paper.

authorHOUSE®

Once there was a little piggy, who had a pretty curly tail.

One day he said, "Mother may I go to the store? I want to buy a red ribbon.
I want to tie it on my pretty tail."

His mother said, "Yes, but you must take the umbrella. It's going to rain."

Piggy said, "Oh no, oh no! It's not going to rain!" And he ran off without it.

But it did rain! The rain poured and poured. It made him dripping wet. He came home crying, because he was soaked to the bone.

His mother said, "Piggy, what a sight you are! Your pretty curl is all gone from you tail."

Piggy said, "Oh dear, oh dear, will it ever curl again?"

Piggy's mother looked at her son, who was so sad because he hadn't listened to his mother.

The next day the sun was shining again, and it was a beautiful day.

Piggy was walking in the woods, still feeling sad.

Then he met a wise old owl.

"Piggy," the owl said, "what happened to your curly tail?"

Piggy told the wise owl how he hadn't listened to his mother, how he had gone to town without the umbrella, and how he got caught in the rain, which had taken the curl out of his tail.

The wise old owl looked at Piggy with his big, brown eyes and stated, "If you do three good deeds for your mother, your tail will curl again."

Piggy was excited, but Mr. Owl cautioned him: "The deeds have to be special, and your mother must not be aware until you finish each deed."

On the way home Piggy thought and thought about the special deeds he could do for his mother.

When Piggy arrived home, he sat down on the porch. Suddenly he noticed something to the right of the house.

Mother's garden was definitely in need of weeding.

Piggy got gloves, a hoe, and a wheelbarrow from the shed.

He began to hoe and pick weeds from the garden.

This is hard work, Piggy thought.

Pretty soon; the wheelbarrow was full, and the garden looked beautiful.

Even Mr. Scarecrow told Piggy how beautiful the garden looked.

Two birds flying by also chirped about how good the garden looked.

Piggy thought hard about the next good deed he could do.

Then it came to him. He could haul all the wood piled by the shed to the back of the house so his mother wouldn't have to haul woods so far.

Piggy grabbed the gloves and the wheelbarrow and began.

This was very hard work, and Piggy was sweating before he was all done.

All the animals; who were watching; cheered when he finished.

Piggy was glad deed number two was finished. He took a bow.

He was already thinking about deed number three.

He would clean his room.

Piggy cleaned and cleaned, and pretty soon everything in his room sparkled.

My mother will be so happy, he said to himself.

Just then, Piggy's mother came into the room.

His mother said, "You sure have worked hard today! The garden is beautiful, the wood is stacked just right, and your room shines! Now, I think, you better get ready for bed."

As Piggy got ready for bed, he kept looking at his tail.

When he was in bed, he checked his tail again. Still no curl.

Piggy tossed and turned all night.

Finally, he fell a-sleep.

When he woke up, the sun was shining, the birds were singing, and the flowers all had their happy faces on.

Piggy looked at his tail, and he couldn't believe it! It was the prettiest tail he had ever seen!

He was so excited, he jumped out of bed and ran straight to his mother.

She was smiling and holding a red ribbon for his tail.